E
GOR

Gorbachev, Valeri.

Chicken chickens.

$16.50

000036064
04/04/2002

DATE		
	WITHDRAWN	

Chicken Chickens

Valeri Gorbachev

A CHESHIRE STUDIO BOOK

North-South Books · New York · London

One fine day, Mother Hen took her two little chickens to the playground for the very first time.

The little chickens were a little scared.
There was so much going on all around them.

They watched two dogs going up
and down on the seesaw.

"Hey, chickens," called the dogs.
"Do you want to play with us?"
"No, thank you," they replied.
"We're just little chickens."

They watched some pigs spinning around on the merry-go-round.

"Hey, chickens," called the pigs. "Do you want to get on with us?"

"Oh, no," they replied. "We might get dizzy. We're just little chickens."

"Hey, chickens," called some big cats.
"Do you want to try the swings?"

"Thanks, but we might fall off," they replied.
"We're just little chickens."

Then the little chickens saw some frogs and mice playing on the slide. Up, up, up they climbed, then *whee!* down they slid.

"Hey, chickens," said one of the mice.
"Climb on up, you're next."
"Oh, no! It's much too scary," they
replied. "We're just little chickens."

"We're little too," said the frogs and mice,
"but we're not afraid. Come on, give it a try."
"Well," said the little chickens. "Maybe . . ."
 and slowly, step by step, they climbed up
 the ladder.

When they reached the top and looked down,
the little chickens were frozen with fear.
"Slide down!" shouted one of the frogs. "Don't be
such chicken chickens!"
"We can't!" cried the little chickens. "We're afraid."

"Don't worry," said Beaver. "Everybody is afraid
the first time they slide. But I have an idea."

"Let's slide together," said Beaver. "Just climb
on my tail and hold tight."

The little chickens held on tight
and closed their eyes.
"*Whee!*" cried Beaver, and down
the slide they went.

"*Whee! Whee!*" cried the little chickens, as they slid off the beaver's tail. "We did it!"

Mother Hen came rushing up. "What's wrong, little chickens?" she asked. "Are you all right?"

"We're fine," said the little chickens. "We went
down the slide and we weren't scared at all!"
"I let them ride on my tail," Beaver said proudly.

"Well, thank you for being so nice," said Mother Hen.

Just then, she heard her little chickens calling. "Look!" they cried. "We're going to slide down all by ourselves!"

And *whee! whee!* that's just what they did!

"Hurrah! Hurrah!" cried all the animals.
"Hurrah for the chicken chickens!"

Wheeee! Wheeee!

First published in the United States, Great Britain, Canada, Australia, and New Zealand
in 2001 by North-South Books, an imprint of Nord-Süd Verlag AG, Gossau Zürich,
Switzerland. Distributed in the United States by North-South Books Inc., New York.
Library of Congress Cataloging-in-Publication Data is available.
The CIP catalogue record for this book is available from The British Library.
ISBN 0-7358-1541-0 (trade edition)
1 3 5 7 9 TR 10 8 6 4 2
ISBN 0-7358-1542-9 (library edition)
1 3 5 7 9 LE 10 8 6 4 2
Printed in Belgium